At the top of a very tall hill in a very small place called Woollybottom, is a horseshoe of houses.

Walter lives in this one

and Winnie lives in that one

which is lucky, because Walter and Winnie are the best of friends.

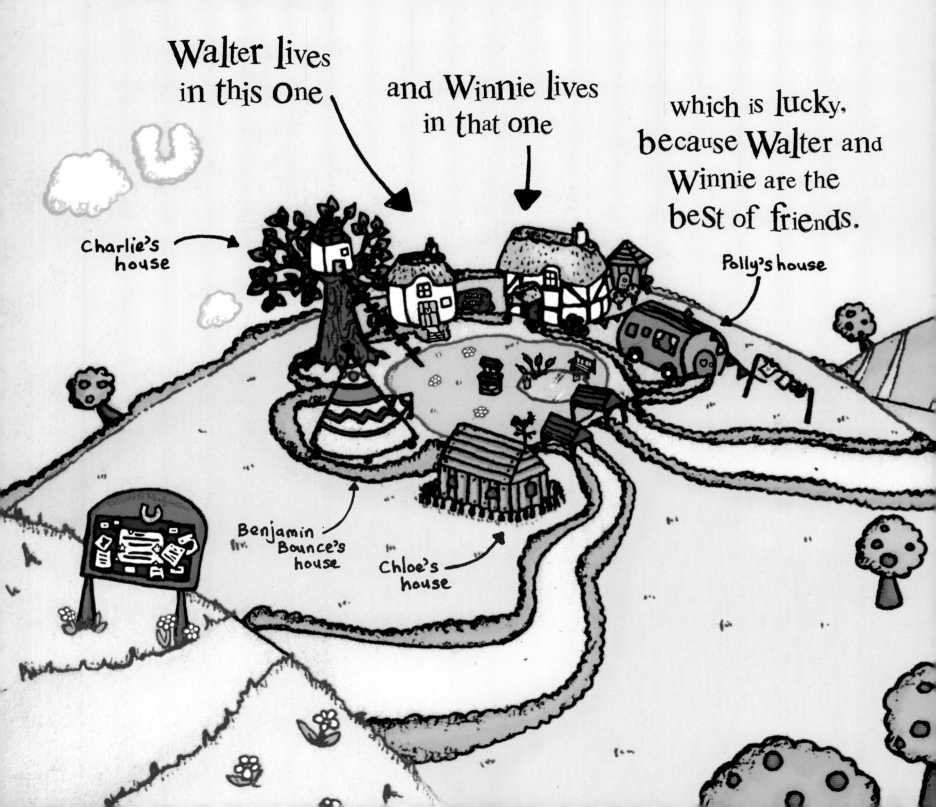

Charlie's house

Polly's house

Benjamin Bounce's house

Chloe's house

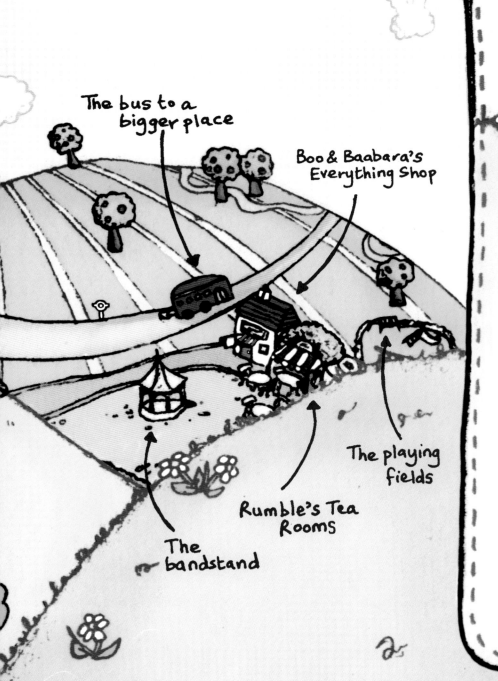

The bus to a bigger place

Boo & Baabara's Everything Shop

The playing fields

Rumble's Tea Rooms

The bandstand

Walter

Winnie

Winnie is happy-go-lucky-top-to-tail Sunshine.

And Walter?

Walter is a worrier. The **biggest** worrier in **Woollybottom**.

Usually, he worries about everyday things like...

the dream he had about a Chocolate-eating monster coming true.

Or...how terrible it would be if he lost Mr. Teddy one day.

Sometimes he even worries that there is something he's forgotten to worry about.

But this story is about the time when Walter's worries got seriously BIG.
Yes, this story is about the week of...

You see, Walter did not particularly like Sport. It made him worry.
But guess what? He'd been picked for not **One**,
not two, but **THREE** events!

Oh my goodness... how this made him **Worry**.

"I bounce SO HIGH and am winning SO MUCH
that my pants Completely COME OFF...
and at that very moment, a TV CREW arrives
and films the no pants thing, and so I am basically
on TV in just my UNDERPANTS!"

Chloe raised a
Cowbrow and Chuckled,
"Don't worry, Walter,
that won't happen."

"It might,"
said Walter.

"I've been picked for the Champion Cheese-Eating event on Sunday, but even though cheese is my **absolute favorite**, I can't possibly do it, because

What if...

"A giant mouse ALSO enters, because he saw me on TV in just my UNDERPANTs. And what if I am SO good at eating cheese that I eat ALL the cheese in the WHOLE UNIVERSE and so he gets really angry and stamps on my HOUSE until it's FLAT!"

Polly and Chloe chuckled.
"Don't worry, Walter, that won't happen," they said.

CHAMPION CHEESE- EATING

"It might,"
said Walter.

Charlie and Benjamin Bounce arrived too.
"Hey, Walter, what's up?" they asked.

"Oh, Charlie! Oh, Benjamin!
I'm supposed to be doing the
Running Quite Fast event on Sunday,
but I can't possibly do it, because

What if...

"I run SO fast
that I don't see
the big hole made
by the GIANT
mouse who saw
me on TV.
And so I fall down
the hole and it goes

THROUGH THE WHOLE
WORLD and I tumble
out into SPACE, where
four ALIENS catch me...

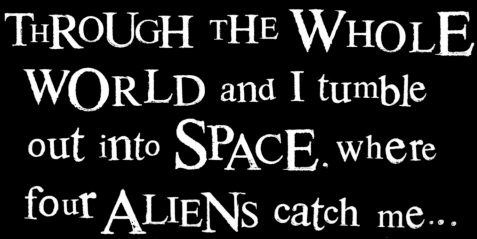

And what if I have to live on their planet forever which you'd think might be lucky because my house is flat, but the only food on the alien planet is bananas...

I HATE bananas!"

"Don't worry, Walter,"
everyone chuckled.
"That won't happen!"

"It might,"
said Walter.

Luckily, just when Walter thought
he might POP with worry, his
bestest friend Winnie arrived.

"What's up, Walter?" she smiled.

"Walter's worried about Sunday,"
said Chloe.

"Walter's worried about EVERYTHING," said Benjamin Bounce.

"No need to worry, Walter, leave it to us!" Winnie said.

Winnie always knew what to do.

And off they went.

EXTRA CRUNCHY CARROTS

CRUNCH YOUR WAY TO SUCCESS

In Winnie's Workshop the Woollybottomers got to work.

They sketched and stitched and glued and hammered and together they hatched a plan to solve Walter's worries.

They had made
Walter his
Very Own...

Worse than that, he couldn't eat **any** cheese because of the anti-giant-mouse-stamping helmet.

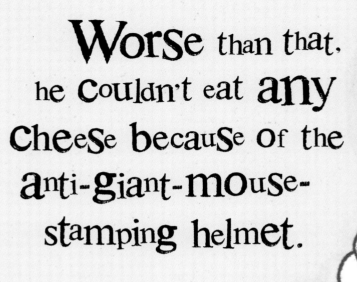

And as for running quite fast...

Well, the magic stay-on pants were **rather** tight, so he got himself in a bit of a pickle...

And whenever Walter was in a pickle, he called Winnie.

"Erm, hi, Winnie," he said. "I'm a little bit stuck about something. I love my new suit, but, I sort of can't do anything properly when I have it on."

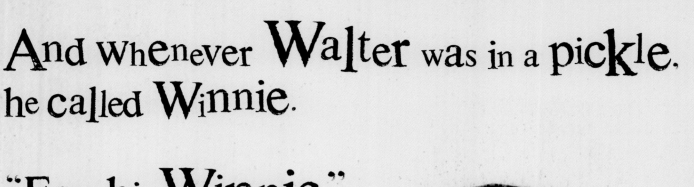

WALTER'S NO-NEED-TO-WORRY SUIT

WHAT IF? / WORST-CASE SCENARIO COMPENDIUM / WHY WE WORRY / AVOIDING SPORT / GLOBAL CHEESE / GOOD LUCK ON SUN

UN-PICKLING YOURSELF & OVERCOMING YOUR WORRIES

NO-NEED-TO-WORRY SUIT instructions

COUNTDOWN TO SPORTS DAY
MON TUES WED THURS FRI SAT SUN

"NO need to worry, Walter." Winnie smiled.

"I know you'll figure out the best thing to do."

But Walter was STILL worrying
When sports day started,
and all the Way through
his first event...

...which didn't go
very well.

AND all the way through his SECOND event,
which didn't go amazingly either...

And Walter was STILL worrying when his very LAST race of the day was about to Start...

"On your marks," said the loudspeaker,

"Get Set..."

SUDDENLY, Walter knew EXACTLY what to do...

"GO!"

He flung off
his Suit... and ran faster
than he'd ever run before!

You see, what this story is really about,
is the time when Walter realized that with
a little help from your friends...

...you can leave
your worries behind you.

THE WOOLLYBOTTOM

WEEKLY TRUMPET

FREE

NEWS FROM A LOVELY PLACE

WALTER WINS!!

1ST

"We always knew Walter could do it," said Winnie, Walter's best friend and spokeshorse for the main Woollybottom crew.

UNDERCOVER MOLE

Morris, our very own undercover journamole reports on the grueling training regime for the running quite fast race.

NEXT WEEK IN WOOLLYBOTTOM:

☆ The Grand Bi-Annual Banquet ☆

NO-NEED-TO WORRY SUIT FOR SALE
AS NEW ☆
(NO LONGER NEEDED)

(SLIGHTLY NIBBLED NON-BANANA SNACKS)

MORE PHOTOS INSIDE......

& OTHER NEWS! ☆

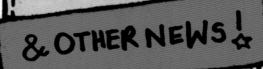

BOO BOUNCES HER WAY TO A NEW WOOLLYBOTTOM RECORD!

NATIONAL CHEESE SHORTAGES

For all the Amazing people
I am lucky enough to Call my friends.
With you in my life. I know for sure
that I haven't a worry in the World.

& with special you-got-me-to-the-finish-line love to
Robbie & Elvis & of course to Mandy, Helen & the whole HC crew.

First published in paperback in Great Britain by HarperCollins Children's Books in 2012
This edition published in 2015
1 3 5 7 9 10 8 6 4 2
ISBN: 978-0-00-758594-6
HarperCollins Children's Books is a division of HarperCollins Publishers Ltd.
Text and illustrations copyright © Rachel Bright 2012
The author/illustrator asserts the moral right to be identified as the author/illustrator of this work.
A CIP catalogue record for this title is available from the British Library. All rights reserved.
No part of this publication may be reproduced, stored in a retrieval system, or transmitted in any
form or by any means, electronic, mechanical, photocopying, recording or otherwise, without the
prior permission of HarperCollins Publishers Ltd. 1 London Bridge Street. London SE1 9GF.
Visit our website at: www.harpercollins.co.uk
Printed and bound in China